Revelling In Him

Damaged, Volume 1

A.B Julian

Published by A.B Julian, 2024.

COPYRIGHT

Synopsis

M/M Romance

Mitchel Carling, the owner of V Carling Hotels and Casinos, never had a doubt about who he is and what he wants. He knows he is selfish and shallow when it comes to relationships. Mitchel has no desire or time to please a partner. Relationships take too much work, and Mitchel is unwilling to put in any effort. He doesn't believe in giving pleasure; he'd rather pay back with money since he got a lot of it than pamper anyone with a dinner and date. An easy transaction, all life's luxuries come with a price tag, so why please a partner with attention?

Jean is struggling to make ends meet. His father left him with a lot of debt that would take his entire life to pay off. He doesn't mind his job, though; it's legal and safe in the state he lives. Jean enjoys giving pleasure. He is not worried about his physical safety, but when he meets Mitchel Carling, the hot billionaire, it's his heart that he is worried about.

Revelling In Him

A. B Julian

Chapter One

Jean

I arrived at the most luxurious hotel in the city. Even though I arrived five minutes early for my appointment, I was still late because it required a unique key to get to the penthouse. So, after frantically searching for a way to reach the penthouse and running through the casinos twice, I returned to the front desk, which I should have done in the first place, but what can I say? I had no experience with such luxurious hotels, and I also had to be mindful of the client's privacy. But what do you know, the receptionist handed me an envelope with my name on it. I ran my hand over my name, "Jean," and it felt pressed in. Why would someone go to such lengths to have an escort's name engraved on an envelope?

I opened the envelope and took out the presidential suite key. The receptionist pointed me in the direction of the correct elevator. I checked the time on my watch and started running – all that felt like a mile or two to the penthouse elevator. I checked myself in the elevator mirror. I undid the top two buttons of my shirt and fixed my dark brown, lightly curled hair. Then I quickly fixed my eyelashes with a colorless mascara to make my already thick and long dark lashes appear prominent, which complimented my light brown eyes. I also used a soft gloss for my lips to give it a wet look.

I felt the air pressure in my ear as the elevator stopped and arrived at the top floor. *Rich people always love to be on top, including the hotel floors.* I searched for the door, thinking there must be a number, which I didn't know since it wasn't on the hotel key. But no, there was no need because there was just one presidential suite on this entire floor. I took a deep breath before I lightly knocked at the door.

"Come in," a very male deep voice ordered and I used the key card to open the door, and let myself in.

The man facing the window had his back to me and was busy pouring himself a glass of what I suspected was very expensive whisky. The man was tall, had long legs and broad shoulders, dark blond hair with the executive cut, and looked hot in those tailored suit pants. After a second, without turning in my direction, he said, "You are late."

"I... well, not technically because I was in the lobby," the man swiftly yet gracefully turned to look at me and gazed at me with amazement like he couldn't believe what he was seeing, and that made me nervous, so I kept on blabbing, "I sort of have never been to, I mean I kind of didn't know that you require a special key to get onto this floor, and there is a separate elevator..."

"You are a man," he interrupted my blabbering, assessing me with that scrutiny.

"I sure hope so," I said with a smile.

"Is this some kind of a joke?" he asked so seriously that I started doubting myself.

"Joke? No Sir. You've ordered ... aa... room service." Classic, I couldn't come up with a better original line. I was seriously fucking this job. It was my first big gig, I was supposed to get paid better and move higher on the ladder than just doing some sloppy Johns, and I was fucking it.

"I asked for a woman!" he said indefinitely.

"Oh," I gave him a nervous smile. Did he want me to dress like a woman? Was that one of his requirements? Joe, my manager, should have told me. "I am sorry, they didn't tell me to dress like a woman. I could probably ..."

"Hold the fuck... I don't want you to dress like a woman. I asked for an actual woman, and Holly High Price said they would send someone named Jean."

"Oh, well, they got the name correct," I said with a nervous smile, and he looked at me like I was a piece of a puzzle he needed to solve. "My name is Jean," I added, and he huffed.

"I am not paying," he said as a matter of fact and then turned to his drink. "I don't get the service, I don't pay," he added.

I knew it was my cue to leave. I didn't want to antagonize a straight client more than I already had because of being a man. It wouldn't go well with HHP or Joe, but I just couldn't help myself.

"But you do get the service." I heard myself say.

He half turned to look at me and checked me out from top to bottom, and I sensed a hint of interest, "You are not a woman," he pointed out again, but he didn't take his eyes off me, and it gave me the courage to move forward.

"I sure am not," I started moving closer. "But I don't think it's a woman you want. You want pleasure, and I am very good at giving just that." I was now in his personal space. It was a risk. A straight man could punch me and beat the hell out of me just for trying that, but he didn't do any such thing and let me undo the top buttons of his expensive shirt as he watched me intently.

I took another risk and placed my wet lips on his collarbone, kissed him, and sucked his skin down to his chest as I continued undoing the buttons of his shirt. When I reached down to his taut packs, I heard him make a huffing sound, then suddenly, holding my shoulder, he pushed me back, halting my movements; he looked straight into my eyes, and I stared into his green dilated pupils. I could see that he was aroused and not conflicted but determined. Using his muscle strength, he pushed me down on my knees.

"You want to please me? I'd start there," he unbuttoned and unzipped his expensive pants while he kept eye contact with me. I smiled and moved to grab his half-hard dick when he grabbed my hair, forcing me to look up, "if you don't make me come, you don't get paid." he warned.

I smiled, "That won't be a problem, Sir," I said.

"So sure of yourself, huh? Let's see how you deliver."

"Yes, Sir," I said as he let go of my hair. Rather than going for the prize, I moved my mouth, kissing and sucking his balls. Right under his shaft, I licked and watched him go fully hard. Oh, he was big, alright. Seeing he was straight, I doubted he was going to fuck me. It would definitely be a shame if he didn't. I brought my focus back to the task at hand as I teased him with my wet mouth, tasting that precum; taking the crown in my mouth, I ran my tongue, making him feel desperate before I sucked him.

"That's a start," he said, and I took pride in his breathless words. "Now, let's see how deep you can take me."

I smiled as I looked up, giving him that seductive look from my thick lashes while I let him watch as I took that long shaft in my mouth. I used my hands to squeeze his balls as I took him all the way back to my throat. I was told my full lips around the cock were a treat. Well, for gay men, but something told me this straight client was sure tasting the piece of this treat.

"Fuck," I heard him say, and I couldn't help but snigger, sending a vibration down his cock. "You are really cocky, aren't you." He said, and he started moving. I pulled my mouth and sucked his crown.

He groaned again, "Enough teasing," he ordered. I looked at him through my lashes and took him in my mouth again, then I let him take control and fuck my mouth, in and out. His hips moved, setting the pace. Then he came hard in my mouth. I let his cum drip through my mouth, and I looked at him, watching his cum dripping down my neck. I didn't swallow, but I still gave the show.

THEN HE PUT HIS COCK inside his expensive pants and zipped himself. He moved to the bar again, sipped his drink, and grabbed some money from the cupboard. He kept it on the bar counter and met my eyes.

"Here's your tip." I stood on my feet and walked to the bar. I looked at the couple hundred-dollar bills. "Since you are not a woman, I can't fuck you. So, that's all you get."

That's all? Was he serious? It was a lot, and it was just a tip; the payment came from Joe.

"Who said you can't fuck me?" I said, meeting his eyes.

"I don't do men," he stated.

"Yet, you just came in my mouth." I challenged.

"That's because I was horney. Any mouth would do."

"Of course, Sir." I smiled, meeting his eyes, I grabbed the cash from the bar. "If you get horney again, you know who to call," I said, leaving his expensive presidential suite.

....

I called Joe and told him what had happened. He checked that another blond girl named Jean was on their roster, and the system had switched our profiles.

"Great, now what does it mean? I am booked with all straight clients?" I asked.

"Don't worry, I'll switch your client list with Jean, the other Jean." He assured.

I got the revised list and locations, none of the clients seemed as rich and most likely not as handsome as that straight client. The girls got all the good stuff.

....

Mitchel

Holly High Price had apologized and promised to send me that beautiful blond girl again at no cost. I didn't want it for free. I wanted the girls to get paid for their service. Prostitution was legal in this state; HHP was licensed and claimed to treat their workers by the code. I took their offer of rebooking but offered to pay.

The woman they sent was pretty and on time. And very submissive, just the way I liked it. But when she got on her knees, I kept picturing that dark-haired man named Jean. He was cocky and so sure of himself and gave a better head. I stopped the girl's sloppy attempts and decided that fucking her would be better. It was okay. I did it because I needed to, but my mind kept picturing that man and how would it feel to fuck him.

The following weekend, I called HHP again. A man named Joe answered and kept apologizing for the mix-up. I asked him if he could send Jean again. It sure shocked him, but he quickly recovered.

"Jean, the boy?" he asked.

"Man," I corrected, "yeah," I confirmed.

"Jean is pretty booked this weekend. Perhaps I can interest you in another lad." He asked.

"No. Does he get booked a lot?" I asked for reasons unknown to me.

"It's the weekend, but I can send...."

Joe continued, and I interrupted, "How about next weekend?"

"Aaaa," he interjected, and when I thought he was going to say no again, he said, "That we can do. Next weekend."

"Okay," I said.

"But what about this weekend? Would you like another girl? Maybe you want to look at some latest pictures?"

"No, thank you. Just book me for next weekend with Jean, and text me confirmation," I disconnected before he could open his mouth again.

....

Chapter Two

Jean

"Hey, Joe, why did you book me next weekend? I had marked my calendar unavailable because I am ..." I called HHP when I got the text for booking.

"It's just a two-hour job, and I will pay you overtime rate." Joe cut me off.

It was tempting; I would love to get paid overtime, but I had promised to help Robbie, my roommate and best friend, with the catering job, and I didn't want to leave him short-handed. Robbie was always there for me and had done a lot for me. "Joe, is everyone else booked?" I asked.

"No, the client specifically asked for you," he said.

"For me? Why?" It intrigued me. I ran a mental list of all my clients.

"How should I know? He just wants you and won't take anybody else. He wanted you this weekend, but you were already booked. So, since I refused him once, I couldn't do it again. He is an expensive client. Now, it has to be next weekend."

I only knew a couple of my clients who would be counted as expensive, and they were closeted husbands; they didn't do weekends.

"So, only two hours?" I asked. I was curious about who this client was.

"Yes, two hours; you think you can work it out?" he asked.

Most weekdays, I worked at the cafe and picked any catering job that was available. Only a few weeknights and Saturdays were when I worked for HHP, but this Saturday, I offered to help Robbie with his catering contract. I'd be two hours away, but I could still help Robbie with loading and offloading at the beginning and end of the shift.

"Okay, fine." I agreed.

"That's my boy," Joe cheered up. "Just so we are clear, I did not pressure you into this. If you want to refuse for any reason, you still can." I smiled at Joe for worrying about legalities.

"No, Joe, you didn't pressurize me. I am okay with it." I confirmed. Most clients at HHP were friendly and had gone through a screening process. They were always required to use condoms, and HHP paid for us to get tested regularly at their private clinic. We got paid by the hours, and the clients decided the hours, but two hours were standard. I didn't want to refuse if I wanted better pay and high clientele; HHP was the safest agency in the city.

"Perfect. I'll text you the address and instructions." Joe said and disconnected. For the client's privacy, we did not get their complete information, only special requests. We only received the exact location in the last hour. I only got to know my client's names if they volunteered that information during our meeting. So, I had no idea who the client was; I had to wait and see ...

.....

The Uber driver dropped me off at the entrance of the hotel. It was one of the most luxurious hotels in the middle of downtown; the other one I had been to for that straight client was also its branch.

"Could it be?" I thought, then shook my head. That straight man wasn't my client, so why would he ask for me? This time, however, instead of searching for the presidential suite entrance, I walked to the hotel lobby and asked them if they had anything for me.

The receptionist handed me the envelope with my name on it. I ran my finger on it, and it felt pressed in. "It is him," I said to myself and couldn't help but smile.

Then, I walked straight to the elevator using the presidential suite card. I made it to the top floor. I felt strange excitement for this client. He was one of a kind, for sure. That rich and handsome man hiring escorts for the company was strange. He sure didn't look like he should have any problem finding a date. Especially when he believed he was straight. Not sure if he still believed that.

I reached the presidential suite and knocked at the door. "Come on in," his all-deep male voice sent feelings to my cock.

I used the key card to open the door. He was again standing near the bar with a drink in his hand. This time, though, he was watching me as I walked in. He checked his wristwatch and then met my eyes again, "At least you are on time," he commented.

"Yes, Sir. But to your disappointment, I am still a man." I said with a smirk.

"I am aware of that." he checked me from top to bottom, stirring a desire inside me. "Now, are you going to stand there all night or get to work." he arched his eyebrows.

I smiled and strolled towards him, and when I tried to step into his personal space hoping for a kiss, he pulled back, "On your knees," he ordered.

I smiled and nodded, then in a graceful motion, I dropped to my knees.

"You are not as needy today. Heard you had a lot of clients," he remarked.

I looked up at him through my dark lashes as I started to unbuckle and unzip his pants and pressed my wet lips on the back of his cock, near his balls. His semi-hard cock was becoming full hard. I licked him, jacked him and ran my tongue on the slit of his crown. He groaned in response. I licked his balls, taking them in my mouth, making him lose his mind. I took his full cock in my mouth and began to suck him. He ran his hand through my hair, which he hadn't done the last time. He hadn't touched me much the last time other than to support his movement. This time, he guided my mouth and controlled the speed. I could tell he didn't want to come so soon. It wasn't his goal today. I sucked the head and squeezed his balls. I knew he was straight or claimed to be, so I didn't go anywhere near his hole. I didn't want him to get angry. He gradually started fucking my mouth, slowly, then faster. Holding my hair in his tight grip, he controlled all the movements, making me hard. I usually didn't get aroused for my clients, but he was stirring desires in me.

"Gonna come," he said, letting go of my hair. He was giving me the option to move back, but I didn't. I let him come into my mouth, and I watched his lustful eyes as he watched his cum drip down my throat. He rubbed his thumb around my lips and cleaned a droplet of his cum. He stared at it on his fingers, then met my eyes again and stepped back. Putting his cock in his pants and zipping up, he went around the bar, and I rose to my feet. This was the time he was going to throw money at me; with any other client, I waited for this moment, but with him, the feelings were different. It was as if I was dreading this moment; the moment I was going to get paid, for the moment I went through all this. I was dreading it.

To my surprise, instead of the money, he took out some napkins and kept on the bar counter, "Clean up," he said, grabbing a glass of wine for himself. "I want you to shower," he said, gesturing towards the bathroom that looked bigger than my apartment.

"Why?" I asked in surprise.

He smiled, looking at me with amusement. "I am your client. I am telling you to take a shower, and you do it." He ordered.

"Yes, Sir." I nodded, took the napkin from the bar counter to clean my mouth and turned towards the bathroom when he said, "wait."

....

Chapter Three

Mitchel

"Wait," I said, and he turned to meet my eyes. "Undress here," I ordered, and he gave me a cocky smile, and I wanted to push his buttons. He started to undo his vest, and I raised my hand to stop him. I could see it riled him a little, but he didn't say anything. "Not like that. Give me a show. The more you entertain me, the higher your tip will be," I smiled, and he frowned at me but said nothing.

Then he smiled, meeting my eyes through his dark lashes and walked toward me. "May I?" he asked, grabbing the controller for the music system.

I nodded in response.

He checked the list on the controller screen and selected "*I'll Make Love to You*," a classic from the list of my already played songs and turned up the volume.

Then, he positioned himself in the middle of the room in front of me. His intense gaze was locked into mine when he smiled, gradually moving his body to the rhythm. He started slow, but his moves were sharp, sliding, shuffling, using his hands and feet in sync. He gracefully moved, performing a dance routine that perfectly matched the beat of the song. His hands touched his vest. He sensually moved his body as he undid his vest. He swung with the rhythm and did a flawless handstand.

I smiled at the movement, it was exciting, and my cock woke to pay attention when he again did a handstand and opened his legs wide in the air. Then, jumping back to his feet, he undid his shirt, walked the imaginary ramp and ran his hand down his chest, making me zero my attention to his flat, slightly muscled stomach.

He came closer, meeting my eyes; he grabbed the bar stool and used it as a tool as he stylishly undid his shoes, one by one. And when the singer sang "Tonight is the night," he danced to the beat, unzipping his pants and taking them off swiftly. He spread his legs in the air again, giving me a full view of his perfect ass. Then he used the wheels of the bar trolley and strolled poised, moving towards me, jumping very last minute to come face to face with me, tilting his head, bringing his mouth closer to mine; he stayed still as the song ended. Our eyes got locked into each other, and neither of us moved. He was slightly out of breath, and I loved how his warm breath touched my mouth. The desire I felt for him was uncanny. Then the song changed, bringing us back to the present, and I stepped back.

"Good show," I said. "Now, shower," I gestured with my head.

He nodded and moved towards the shower; being painfully aware of his nakedness, I took the opportunity to admire his back, those long, slender legs, and those perfect hips were beautiful.

......

Jean

I bathed in that expensive hotel soap and took my sweet time with that perfectly tempratured hot water. I knew he was waiting. He wanted me clean, so he could fuck me. Part of me wanted to tease him, ask him what changed, didn't he say he only fucked women. But I wasn't allowed to question a client. And I wasn't risking this job just because I wanted to tease him. If an expensive client like him complained, that'd be the end of it.

I stepped out of the shower and dried myself using a hotel towel while I checked myself in the mirror. My cheeks looked flushed, and my hair were wet. I tried to dry them while I looked around for some product for a quick dry. My eyes scanned the amenities in the walk-in space; there was a perfume in the mix with other hotel amenities. It was sure his. I picked it up. I didn't recognize the brand, I opened it. It smelled so good, just like him, rich and expensive. When I got lost in the smell of his perfume, I didn't notice him enter the bathroom. He stepped right behind me, and through the mirror, my brown eyes met his green eyes that were surrounded by dark blond lashes. He was damn good-looking. It was just icing that he was taller than me. Pulling me closer, he wrapped his arm around my naked chest. He rubbed his lips under my ear, kissing my neck, moving down my shoulder—making me close my eyes with need.

"I've never been so aroused for a man," he whispered behind my ear, his breath giving me goosebumps.

"I take it you liked the show," I remarked, meeting his eyes again, and he smirked.

"I want to fuck you," he said, and my cock stirred involuntarily. He chuckled, "I see your dick likes the idea."

"It sure loves sex," I replied, acting nonchalant.

He grabbed the perfume bottle from my hand, which I'd forgotten I was still holding. He gently sprayed it on my chest, then sniffed my neck, moved his nose in my hair, his lips touching my nape. "Smells good on you," his voice deep and sexy and full of need. "Talking about sex, we need to set some rules." he met my eyes in the mirror again.

"I am listening," I said, keeping the eye contact.

"Other than the basic HHP rules, is there anything you don't like? You don't want me to do?" he asked.

The question took me by surprise. No one ever asked me that before. I saw that he was waiting for me to say something, "Umm, I am okay with a little rough, but I am not into BDSM, not even handcuffs, no restraints, nothing." I turned my face to the side to say to him directly.

"Okay," he said, still looking in the mirror.

"If you want me to use a toy. I'll have to see it first," I added, meeting his eyes in the mirror again.

"Noted," he said. "Anything else?" he asked, and I shook my head in response.

"It's my first time with a man, so if I hurt you, you have to tell me. At any time, you feel you don't want to do this. You have to tell me to stop, no hesitation, no obligation. You can tell me to stop at any time for any reason, personal or professional. I won't question you. I will still pay you and will not complain to your agency. You are not my prisoner. You are free to leave at any time. You understand me?"

"I understand," I said.

"Good. Now, let's see you spread those long legs again in my bed." His lips rubbed my cheeks while he spoke, raising a new desire in me. I turned, getting out of his arms, I walked towards the door, then I stopped at the door, giving him a full view of my body. I smiled as I met his eyes and walked back to his bedroom. The bed was huge, and the room was enormous, facing the terrace. I sensed him come into the room. I turned to face him again and sat on the edge of the bed then moved back, gradually spreading my legs, just like he wanted. I saw the hunger in his for me, and it made me proud. I moved and grabbed the lube from the side table. I rested my head on the pillow and generously applied lube on my fingers, then, spreading my legs wider again, put a lubed finger inside my hole. All this time, I kept my eyes on him, he was intently watching all my moves, and I could see the bulge in his pants. Oh, he really wanted to fuck me, alright. No hesitation of a straight man, no panic, no self-doubt; he was so sure of himself. It was a turn on to watch him watching me prepare myself for him.

As I massaged my hole with that lube, he started to undo his shirt's buttons one at a time, and then he undid his cuff links, all while he never took his gorgeous green eyes off me. Leaving his shoes on the side, he undid his pants. I rubbed my cock as I watched him, and his eyes moved from my hands to my eyes. He didn't take off all his clothes. He walked towards me and sat next to me on the bed.

"Little, desperate are we?" He smiled, coming closer and meeting my eyes, "Don't touch your cock." He ordered and moved to push my hand away while I removed my hand, and his hand landed on my cock, making me moan desperately. He stared at my cock in his hand, then he smiled and jacked me a little, enough to make my hips buckle up. "Don't come," he ordered. I groaned and forced myself down, and he chuckled. Then he focused his eyes on my cock again; he moved his hand down from my cock, grazing my balls, he pushed a finger inside my hole, and I moaned with need. I mostly had to fake it with other clients, but I was enjoying myself today. It didn't even feel like a job. He was so focused on fingering me, like he was exploring me, wanting to know everything about my body, like a lover would. I moaned when his fingers reached my prostate. And his eyes moved to my face, "You like that?" He asked.

"Yes, Sir," I said, and he smiled, rubbing his fingers some more, and I grew more desperate. Then he stopped, and I wanted to beg him to keep going, but when he started to remove his pants and shirt again, I took an eyeful of his naked body. He had zero fat, was lean but muscled, and must have never skipped the gym or a pool. He sure had a swimmer body. With those strong arms and legs, he climbed onto the bed again. This time, he positioned himself between my legs, and I forced myself to control and not come all over him. "Anytime now, Sir," I said, and he chuckled at me; he grabbed the condom from the side table and suited up.

"You are really that desperate to be fucked?"

"Hmm, you have no idea."

He smirked, but he finally placed his big cock between my legs, and I moved forward to get it a little deeper, and he held my arms, holding me in place, "No, Jean," he moved above me to look into my eyes, I couldn't move even if I wanted to, he was strong, "I do this and don't worry, I'll make sure you enjoy." He said, and I bit my lips while he pushed my legs up and started to fill my hole with his thick cock. And it felt good. He started moving in and out, finally hitting my prostate, and I groaned with need. "I guess I found your sweet spot." He said, kissing my earlobe.

"You can go a little faster. I won't break, Sir, I promise."

He chuckled in response, "Okay, you asked for it."

He grabbed my hips a little tighter and pushed harder. "Oh fuck," I yelped.

"Okay? Keep going?" He asked, trying to meet eyes that I could barely keep open.

"Oh please, don't stop," I said, and he laughed again.

"You are needy, and I fucking love that," he said and started fucking me harder and faster. And it felt so good. "I am gonna come." He said, and then he grabbed my cock and massaged it, and it was enough encouragement I needed. I came in his hands, it squeezed my ass around his cock, and I felt him come inside me, filling that condom. He groaned in reaction. While he fucked me with a few more strokes to my cock in his hand, we were both spent. Then he lied beside me, catching his breath. "Wow, that was good, better than I imagined."

I snickered, "Told you, should have given me a chance the first time." And he laughed.

"No, this is perfect, needed that build-up." He said.

"Yeah, there is that," I said, and our eyes got locked into each other, and we both didn't move for a few stretched seconds and then his eyes flickered to my lips; he quickly looked away, his eyes now focused on the ceiling like he was thinking of redesigning its pattern. "I left your tip at the counter; don't forget before you leave," he spoke without looking at me, and I knew I was being dismissed. I got off his bed since I was no longer welcome there. "Oh, and Jean," he called, and my name in his deep voice made my heart speed up.

I turned to face him, "yeah?" I asked.

"Leave that key card at the counter. Last time, you forgot."

I nodded, "Yes, Sir, won't forget this time." I swiftly made my way to the bathroom and quickly cleaned myself, and when I came out, he wasn't there; then I heard a shower in another bathroom.

Apparently, I wasn't even worth a goodbye. I grabbed my clothes off the floor, dressed quickly, picked up the money, left the key card and got out of there fast.

......

Chapter Four

Jean

"Skinny Cafe Latte, just as you like it." Robbie chimed, keeping my drink at the counter.

"Thanks," I said, handing him the cash.

"You get the employee benefits now; remember, it's free," Robbie reminded me, handing my cash back.

"Oh, yeah, I forgot," I smiled. Robbie had helped me get the job here. I'd spend most of my weekdays working here, which will help me pay off the rent.

"Rough night?" He asked. Robbie knew what I did for money; he was my insurance. The arrangement was that if I didn't show up here every morning for the latte or answer my phone, he would call the cops and give them my manager's contact to find me. Holly High Price was safe, but it's not like they could be sure of all clients being gentlemen. Every night was a risk. "Bad client?" He whispered to me.

"No, the client was pretty good. I mean, he paid me a good tip."

"Great. So, what's the problem." He probed.

"There is no problem," I smiled. "Everything is good, perfect." I took a sip from my latte and cheered at him.

He smiled and nodded.

Everything was perfect. He paid me more in tips than HHP paid me for the actual job. HHP took the bigger cut, but they promised safety and high-end clients. We could put down our preferences in our profile, and the system never paired me with a client with a BDSM fetish, so that was a blessing. Also, all their clients were instructed to use condoms, and we were told we could refuse at anytime. Of course, the last was mostly on paper; if you did refuse it, you wouldn't get the next call that quickly; the algorithm on their website would push your profile down and mark you as unreliable. Still, I couldn't complain; Joe had been good so far at finding me clients. Most were closeted married men with too much collateral damage; they were the safest. And then there was this presidential suite guy. I didn't see a wedding band other than the ring on the last finger of his right hand; it looked more like a family heirloom than a relationship promise, but there was no way he was single; a good-looking and rich guy like that would have no problem finding a date. I don't know why I felt so bad for being dismissed after the hot sex we shared. He was, after all, a client, just a client. I might never see him again, anyway. Now that he got his curiosity out of the way, he didn't need to ask for me again.

....

Mitchel

I read through all the legal papers the lawyer had sent for filing for our new hotel location, and now my eyes were swimming. This week was busy. We had to submit a blueprint twice for approval. It got rejected the first time. The land required an extra layer for protection; the depth wasn't good enough. This time, I made sure I checked everything myself. No matter how competent they are, you can't leave anything to the staff; it's your neck on the line.

I was rereading the guidelines for the state laws for building when my computer dinged with a new email. It was from Holly High Price, they had sent their latest catalogue. My mind quickly flashed back to Jean.

He intrigued me; he was fun. And wow, just the thought of him could make me horney. It hadn't happened in a long time. Maybe because he was a man, something new was exciting.

I opened the email, and it took me to their website. I entered the password, where I got the exclusive list of their escorts. There were a couple of new girls. They were pretty, but not what I wanted. I went into my profile setting and selected the option of men and women 22 to 30. I didn't like them too young. It prompted me to choose the body type and preferences for the male escort. I made my choices. I only wanted one. I'd never been into threesome. I liked to be in charge. When it came to selecting body type, I noticed that I had selected Jean's body type: slender, slightly muscled, and fit. I didn't care about height. I first only selected brunette because of Jean's hair, then I also selected blond and red. All colour types should be okay.

Then there was this section for fetish. My mouse hovered over the handcuffs. Jean said it was an absolute no for him, but I occasionally enjoyed it. I could picture Jean in the handcuffs, in my bed, looking all sexy and at my mercy, but it wasn't possible since he didn't like it. I selected a few toys but didn't have much experience with them. Maybe it was different with men. After saving my preferences, I refreshed the catalogue. It showed me a few attractive young men. I kept scrolling down to the next page, and then next, they were not what my eyes were searching. Then I went back to my profile and unchecked the handcuffs and toys. I refreshed the catalogue again, and then finally, there he was on page seven, "Jean," I read his profile. He was twenty-six, and he liked to dance and party. He was a gymnast, so he was very flexible. I had the pleasure of witnessing that. I scrolled through his pictures. His brown eyes were beautiful, and his golden skin had a natural tan. He was of Latino and Italian heritage. I examined his pictures again; one showed him shirtless, another was a headshot,

My mouse hovered over the Book Him icon. I clicked on his picture again and stared into his beautiful light brown eyes and those perfectly symmetrical lashes around his eyelids. He gave off a look of vulnerability; of course, that could just be a pose, a job requirement. It was appealing, for sure.

I clicked on the Book Him icon, and it opened a warning screen; for no BDSM rule, there were options for other similar-looking men who offered that service. I clicked on the I accept the rules. And it took me to pick the date. He wasn't available this Saturday. I huffed and picked up the phone to call HHP. After selecting AI options that verified my information, a man named Joe answered on the first ring.

"I want to book Jean for this Saturday," I said.

"Of course, Sir, let me just check." I waited, and after some time, he spoke again. I am sorry, Sir, he is already booked. May I interest you another lad?"

"No," I said, but I didn't hang up. "Can't you switch his other client's booking with me?" I asked.

"Aww, I'll just check on that. Can I put you on hold?" He asked.

"Okay," I said and listened to the stupid music, their repeated message about client safety and privacy, and all the promises of pleasure when he finally picked up the phone again.

"Sorry for the wait, Sir. I cleared Jean's schedule, and he is all yours for the two hours on Saturday night."

"Okay, thank you."

"You are most welcome; thank you for..." he kept going, but I disconnected.

I also went back on the website and booked him for next Saturday. Just to be safe. I didn't want to overthink my actions, so I went back to reading the government's guidelines for building.

....

Jean

I got a notification on my phone that my Saturday booking was cancelled. I called Joe right away.

"Hey, my booking got cancelled in less than 24 hours. Do I still get paid?"

"No, your booking is not cancelled; there's some change. I'll send you an update."

"Okay," I said, and Joe disconnected, and a new booking showed up with a new location. And I knew who he was, and the thought brought an involuntary smile to my lips.

....

Chapter Five

Jean

When I reached his presidential suite door and knocked before I could put in the key, he opened the door for me.

He nodded to me to come on in; he was on the phone, so I kept quiet. "I need to finish this; you mind taking a shower." he pointed at the bathroom.

"Sure," I nodded. "It's not like I was clean or anything," I muttered to myself.

"You've said something?" he held the phone to his chest and asked.

"No, Sir. Taking a shower." I quickly moved, and I heard him get back to his phone.

"Yeah, Mitchel here." I heard him say on the phone. So, his name was Mitchel. At least now I could call him Mitchel in my head. "Of course I'll attend it, what kind of question is that?" I heard him say on the phone before I turned on the shower. The water was a treat, though.

When I came out of the shower, I heard the door. I dried myself quickly, checked who it was at the door, and saw the waiter setting up the dinner table.

What? He is expecting company. The information didn't say anything about a threesome. I didn't like it, but I couldn't deny it; all HHP could do was charge double. I decided to make it clear to him. I watched the waiter leave. No one else entered the room, so I wrapped the towel around my hips and walked back to him.

....

Mitchel

I watched Jean come out of the shower; his dark hair were wet, and his skin was glistening. My eyes zeroed on his hairless chest and pink nipples.

"Sir, if you are expecting a company, I'd have to charge extra for another, and I'd have appreciated it if I had been told in advance." he looked worried.

"Come again?" I didn't understand for a second, then I realized he looked worked up over the dinner table.

"Are you expecting someone else to join us?" he asked.

"No, I am not expecting another company," I said, taking a seat at the dinner table. "I didn't eat all day, so I ordered some food. Join me. Have a seat." I moved his plate in front of him. He looked shocked and just stared at me. "Sit down, Jean," I ordered, and then he finally moved to take a seat. "Do you like stake? I have nothing vegan or vegetarian, but if you want, I can order."

"No, this is good. Thank you." he drank the water like he was dying of thirst. This was the first time I saw him nervous, and it gave me a smile.

"Don't fill yourself." I interrupted his drinking, he stared at me in question. "You need to eat," I reminded him.

I took a bite from my stake. It was good, and I watched him eat; he made a pleasured noise, making me chuckle.

"Sorry," Jean said, "this is really good."

"I sure hope so. The chef is a fucking diva." I muttered more to myself than him. When he stared at me confused, I added, "Never mind, want some wine?"

He nodded.

I took the red wine and poured it for both of us. I watched him take a sip, and his lips glistened in the colour of the wine. His lips looked soft, his flawless skin and his wet hair were a temptation.

"Your hair look nice," I touched his soft brown hair and felt his head lean into my hands. "Feel So soft." I admired it, running my fingers through it.

He smiled, "Must be the hotel's shampoo," Jean said.

"That's my shampoo. If I'd put that for hotel guests, I'd have to charge them triple the fee. "I took a sip from my wine and saw him watching me. "All done?" I asked, looking at his plate. He had cleaned it. Seemed like he was hungrier than I was.

"Yeah." he said, taking a sip from the wine, "it was really good." he gave me a pure smile, not his cocky look.

"I want you to sit on my lap," I demanded. He looked at me through his thick lashes, got up from his seat, and came close. I removed his towel, and was happy to see him aroused for me. I turned him around and helped him sit. I inhaled his scent and rubbed my erection through my pants between his naked asscheeks, then I ran my hand against his smooth chest and rubbed my thumb around his nipple; he made a needy sound. So, I rubbed his nipples again and felt them becoming hard. I kissed his nape and started to unbutton my pants. He gave me room to unzip and take out my cock as he settled back down on my naked cock. I groaned.

"Sir. I am not a girl. I need supplies," he breathed.

That made me laugh; with his dick in my hands, could he ever think I would mistake him for a girl.

"I think girls need supplies, too. Turn around." I instructed. He got up from my lap and turned. "Put your legs around me." he looked worried but followed my command. I took out a lube sachet and condom from my pocket and kept it on the table. "I've got supplies." I said.

He bit his lip to hold his smile. Seriously, that made him happy; he seemed more in spirit.

He moved to take the lube, but I held his hand, "No," I took the packet from his hand, "I'll do it." I added lube to my hand, moved my hand between his stretched legs and put a finger inside his hole. His hands automatically settled on my shoulders, and I pulled him closer; his cock rubbed against mine, and that was a sensation I never experienced before. I wanted more. I pushed my finger inside him, then I took his nipple in my mouth, and I felt his fingers tighten around my shoulders. His pleasure was a reward. He was an enigma. I loved his reactions. It turned me on as much as when I fed him my cock. I never gave pleasure. I always thought it was a relationship obligation. This way, I paid back with money and didn't have to please them, but with Jean, giving him pleasure was a pleasure. I fucked him with my fingers, just as I had seen him do it to himself the other night. I could see he barely held himself when I touched his prostate a few times. His breathing was uneven, but he was trying to control it.

"I think I am ready, I need your cock, Sir. Unless you want me to come on your hands," he breathed out the words.

Tempting, but I needed to fuck him. I took out my fingers and let him relax a little. Grabbing the condom off the table. After suiting up and lubing my shaft, I then grabbed his legs, lifted him, and adjusted him on my cock. He used the chair to settle on my cock. I could see he didn't want to put all his weight on me.

I wrapped my arm around his waist and pulled him down, "It's okay, you can use me. Now, you set the pace." I told him and felt his hole wrapping around my cock. I wanted him to use his need for pleasure to guide his pace. He placed his arms around my shoulder and his chest right next to my face. I wanted to suck his nipples again, but I did not want him to lose focus.

I supported him with my arms and hands around his hips as he gradually started moving. Slow at first, his tight muscles felt good around my shaft. I felt him seeking his own pleasure when he went deeper, and that was the pleasure I needed. It was so damn hot. I rubbed my hand on his back, feeling his soft, smooth skin, running my hand through his soft hair. He smiled, looking into my eyes with those dilated pupils as he picked his pace. I groaned with need, and our breathing got mingled into each other.

"Fuck, you are hot." I breathed out and felt his muscle squeeze my cock when he sputtered his load on me, and I came inside him, filling that condom. I thought for a moment about how it would feel without a condom, but that wasn't a possibility. It was a rule I was never going to break.

We stayed in that position, and then he grabbed a napkin and started to clean his cum off my shirt.

"It's okay," I said, halting his hand. I held his legs and helped him get off me, but I could feel his legs were wobbly, so I helped him sit in his chair. Then I just watched him. He looked all red and warm. Then I touched his flushed cheeks to feel the warmth, and he met my eyes through his lashes, "You are pretty." I said, and I could see my compliment surprised him, maybe because this was the first time I complimented his beauty.

My watch chimed, interrupting our gaze. It was a meeting reminder I had to meet my brother and his bride-to-be at the nightclub. "I have to go." I quickly rose to my feet, adjusting my pants. I took out the envelope from the drawer with his tip in it and kept it on the table in front of him, "You can shower if you want. I am using the other bathroom." I told him. He still hadn't taken his eyes off the envelope when I went to the bathroom. And he was gone when I came out of the bathroom. His absence made me feel strange like I was missing him already.

....

I again booked him for next Saturday and Saturday after that. It had become a routine. I looked forward to my weekends with Jean. It was fun watching him become undone with my touch when I fucked him real hard, and he looked like he couldn't move. I lay beside him, pulled him in my arms, and stared at the ceiling while we caught our breath. It felt good lying next to him, not doing anything but knowing he was right beside me like he was mine. My phone chimed, breaking the magic.

Jean

HE HAD HELD ME CLOSER after sex, giving me the feeling of belonging, like I was his. I knew I was in trouble. I couldn't let myself fall for him. I nowhere belonged in his rich world. Right now, though, I didn't want to worry and just enjoy these little moments of happiness with Mitchel.

"Fuck," I heard him say. He was checking his phone. He sat up and called someone. "Did you upload the documents?" He asked. The other person said something. "I told you to upload the document on the server before you send them out." The other person was mainly apologizing. "Send it to me right now." He instructed but not so nicely and disconnected the call. Then he called someone again, "Hey Jessica," this time he sounded so charming. Yeah, Mitchel here. My assistant sent you the contract." I could hear Jessica say that she got it. "Can you just hold them off for a day? They might be okay, but I need to check some things." She sounded like she agreed. "Thank you, you are sweetheart," He said some more nice things before he disconnected.

"Can you believe these people? They can't follow simple instructions," he again wrapped his arm around me while he was checking his phone, and I realized that he was talking to me. He never talked to me about anything but sex, which gave my stupid heart false hopes.

"Are you a lawyer?" I asked mainly to distract my heart from believing it was anything more than just a random conversation.

And, he laughed. "No, do I look like a lawyer?" He said pleasantly.

"You were talking about contracts, so I thought." I had heard him talk about cases, filing and contracts when he was on the phone.

"No, I am a businessman. In a business, you have to know all the codes and laws and don't even get me started on the amount of tax law you have to know. I guess it makes me half-lawyer. I studied business in college, though."

I nodded, thinking about it, picturing him doing all that work.

"What about you? Finished college?" he asked.

"Umm, no, dropped out," I said.

"You can still go back and finish it. What were you taking?" he asked, and his phone rang. This time, he grabbed it and went to the bathroom, breaking whatever connection he was unintentionally building. Next time, he wouldn't even remember this conversation. I got out of his bed to get dressed to leave.

....

Mitchel

"So, are we finalizing the design? Do you think we should add any extra features?" Gupta asked.

I again checked the 3D model of our new hotel's blueprint.

"Looks good," I said.

"Yeah, it goes with the location and is within the chain's signature look," Gupta highlighted the pattern.

"Gupta, you are gay, right?" I blurted and then realized my question might not fly with HR. Gupta was my employee, and I probably asked an inappropriate question. "If you don't mind me asking, you can refuse to answer." I quickly added.

Gupta laughed, "Now I am sure curious what thought process led to this question? And to ease your mind, yes, I am openly gay and don't mind the question."

"It's probably not appropriate to ask," I said.

"Only if you make a sexual advance at me. You are my boss, and I am in a committed relationship." he showed me his ring. I smiled at that.

"No, I am not making a move on you. I just have a few questions, and I just don't know who to ask."

"Well, as long as your questions are not homophobic in nature," he arched his eyebrows.

"No, absolutely not," I assured him.

"No offence, but many straight men don't realize when they're being a douch."

"Oh no, it's not like that. It's about me. I have developed an interest in another man."

"Oh, okay," He looked surprised but tried to hide it. "In that case. I am all ears. We could grab some drinks after work and talk about it."

"I'd appreciate that," I said and returned to checking the blueprint.

....

"So, Mitchel Carling is into men. I have to admit I am surprised, and no offence. I mean, I should know. We don't have a dress code," he said, and I laughed.

"Not precisely into men. It's just this one man." I corrected.

"Like first time?" he asked.

"Yeah, and I never had any interest in any other man and here is what I want to know: when does it get over?"

"What do you mean?" He asked.

"Okay, can I be blunt?" I asked.

"Sure, you are talking to a gay man; there is nothing I never heard before."

I laughed, "Good to know."

"So, I have been sleeping with this man,"

"You want to say you've been fucking this man," he suggested.

I chuckled, "Yes, exactly."

"Okay, so?"

"So, I thought if I do it a few times, I'd be over him, but every time, it feels like it's not enough."

"So, you want it to be over?" He asked, searching my face.

"Yeah, I never had such a problem with any woman, and I think it's because he is a man, and it's about that added pleasure of I don't know what?" I took a sip from my drink.

"Okay. so if you think it's only about him being a man, maybe try meeting another man."

"I've tried, but I just keep going back to him."

He laughed.

"Don't laugh. I want your expertise. I assume you've been gay for long, so you must have been with many men." I said.

"I have." He smiled proudly.

"So, tell me, when do you get over one man so you can fuck another?"

"How many times have you fucked him?"

"More than a few," I said.

"And you still crave him?"

"I said that already; this is the problem we are discussing," I said, and he laughed again.

"Okay, I'd been with many men, and I got over them pretty much the same way you got over the woman you described in your life."

"Okay," I said, listening intently.

"But there were only two men in my life I couldn't get over no matter how many times we fucked. One was in college when we broke up; it took me years to recover," he stared at his drink in his hand.

"And the other one?" I prompted when he didn't speak.

"The other is the one I am married to," He showed me his ring again.

I stared at his ring and dared ask,"What are you saying?"

"I am saying there is no formula for it, Mitchel. It's not about him being a man and not a woman; it's about him, period."

"No, it's not the same." I denied sipping my drink again and not paying attention to my heartbeat, which raced as if it was catching me in a lie.

"Maybe your body is saying that this man is forever for you, but your mind is not accepting it. In that case, I suggest taking a break from him. Either your body catches up with your mind, or your mind catches up with your body." He said, finishing his drink and ordering another one.

I thought about it. I could take a break from Jean. It didn't have to be this Saturday; just one more night with Jean wouldn't hurt.

....

Chapter Six

Mitchel

I stepped onto the terrace of my room. The weather was perfect, not too hot, and there was a nice cool summer breeze. I could see the city lights. I asked the server to set up the dinner table on the terrace before Jean arrived. Seeing that he enjoyed stake, I ordered a lamb leg. It was the chef's specialty. The meat was always tender and mouth-watering. It was last night with Jean, and I wanted to make it special. I knew Jean would like it. I smiled at myself, thinking of Jean as I poured red wine into my glass. Then, there was a knock at the front door.

"Come on in," I said using the intercom, and he used the card to get in. He always wore the same white shirt, black jeans, and black vest. He also wore a bit of makeup, which usually washed when he took a shower, so I didn't know why he bothered. He was pretty as he was. "I am here," I said when his eyes searched for me in the room. Then he smiled when he saw me, and my heart sped. I tried to ignore it. It was just excited for the promised sex, I told myself and continued watching Jean as he joined me on the terrace.

"I thought we'd have dinner here tonight." I gestured for him to sit. But he didn't move.

"Don't you want me to shower first?" he asked.

"Maybe later. Jean. Take a seat." I ordered. And he sat quickly.

I smiled and opened the dish, "I ordered lamb. Do you like it?" I asked, cutting out a piece for him."

"I never had it," He said.

I smiled at that, "Hmm, then you are in for a treat." I placed the piece on his plate and cut one for myself.

"Umm, this is really good, like heaven," he made that sexy sound again.

I smiled and took a sip from my wine glass. I watched him eat ravenously, and it was a delight.

He moaned again, mixing the lamb with mashed potatoes. "You know, I worked at a restaurant once, but they never cooked anything like this, but then we didn't have any rich people come in there. Most customers came for hot dogs or fajitas."

"So, you think rich people don't eat fajitas and hot dogs?"

He sniggered, "No, I mean you would never step into that restaurant. It was a corner restaurant in between two streets in the lower town. Your car wouldn't even fit in that street," he smiled as he took another bite.

"You don't know what car I drive," I said.

"I am pretty sure you take a limo everywhere you go." I opened my mouth to argue, but my eyes zeroed on his lips when he ran his tongue around it.

"Can I taste that?" he asked, looking at the chocolate cake dessert, and I noticed that he had finished his meal.

"Yes, it's all yours. I don't like dessert." I placed it in front of him.

"But you ordered one?" he started cutting a piece but met my eyes when he asked.

"I ordered for you. You said you like chocolate," I said, and his eyes lost a little light.

"I never said that. You must be mistaking me for someone else," he lowered his eyes as he spoke.

"You didn't?" I could have sworn that I knew Jean liked chocolate.

Then he smiled, and his eyes sparkled, "You read my profile," he said.

And I flushed at the way he gave me that cheeky smile.

"Maybe. That's how I choose." I shrugged. It wasn't a secret.

"By researching that they like a dessert that you don't?" His cheeky smile was back.

"No, researching for allergies. don't want anyone allergic to latex." I shrugged, acting nonchalantly.

He laughed, and I noticed that it was the first time I heard his carefree laughter, which was soothing. "I don't think any prostitute in the history of prostitution ever claimed that they are allergic to latex. That'd be bad business." He took another big bite from the cake, and he looked beautiful. He looked at me from his plate, meeting my eyes, and I couldn't help but stare into his golden eyes; at that moment, I felt a strong pull toward him, like I wanted him to be mine so no one else could ever touch him. Then He lowered his eyes, breaking the eye contact, "I am sorry, you didn't want me to use that word?" he looked all worried; all his lightness and humour were gone.

I shook my head and smiled, "More wine?" I offered. I didn't wait for his answer and filled his glass.

Then, I grabbed my glass and walked to the terrace railing. I looked across the skyline and admired the city lights.

After a minute, Jean came and stood beside me. I could smell his cheap perfume, which left a bad taste in my mouth.

"I am sorry if I said something." he apologized again.

"Did you have someone else today? Another client?" I questioned, looking at him sideways.

"I AM SORRY, I AM NOT allowed to discuss that." he lowered his eyes. I took another sip from my glass and stared at the night light, and after a significant pause, he added, "But no, I haven't been with anyone else today." After another long silence, when I was about to take another sip from my glass, he asked, "Do you want me on my knees?"

My hands stilled for a second as I gazed at the skylight, and then I placed my wine glass on the top rail and turned to face him. I met his beautiful brown eyes, and then my eyes fell on his sensuous lips that still glistened with red wine. Then I stepped forward, holding his face. I tasted his lips, putting my lips between his; I felt the softness and texture of his lips. My fingers moved into his soft hair, controlling his movement. I pushed my tongue inside his mouth, tasting red wine, chocolate and a taste of just him. His hands came to rest on my back, and his body moved closer. I placed my other hand on his hips and pulled him closer, forcing his body to touch every part of mine as I kissed him harder. I could feel his erection against my legs, and I pushed him against the terrace wall. I quickly undid his pants and took out his cock, and massaged it while I kissed him some more. I used my tongue to fuck his mouth while I squeezed his balls and kept jacking him, his body moved against my hands, and I could feel his desperation with how his body clung to mine. He came in my hands fast and hard, and I didn't let go until he was all spent.

Then I let go of him and stepped back to look at him. He was breathless, his lips looked swollen and abused, he barely stood on his feet, he looked used, and it was gratifying. "Now, let's take that shower," I said and didn't wait for him to follow.

.....

Jean

It took me time to recover from what had just happened. That kiss turned me on so much it was painful, and when did Mr. Presidential Suite kiss me? I thought he was aversive to my mouth, as if he found me dirty. But today was? What? I followed him into the bathroom. He was already in the shower. Was I supposed to join him? He opened the shower door and said, "You are gonna stand there all night? Come on in." he ordered. I quickly started to strip. He rested his back on the shower wall as he observed me strip. I also watched how the water from the shower fell on him, and he ran his hand through his hair, like a movie star in a shampoo commercial. There was no denying he was hot as hell. But he was also wealthy, and that made him off-limits. He was just a client. I reminded myself he looked through the door and gestured with his finger for me to come in.

I gradually moved into the shower with him. It was big enough for four people, with two separate showers. He turned on the other shower when I entered. The water was warm but not hot. It felt perfect against my hot skin. He watched me, moved closer, pressed the bottle of soap, generously poured it into his big hand, and carefully rubbed it against my chest. Then he turned me and rubbed more soap on my back, then ran his finger between my ass cheek, massaging me; he wrapped his arm to my chest and pulled me against his body. I felt his hard cock behind me. He cleaned my cock, rubbing it a few times, enough to make me hard again. Then he shut off the water, grabbed the towel and dried us quickly.

"In my bedroom," he said, holding my hand. He guided me all the way to his bed and pushed me onto his mattress, then he moved on top of me and kissed me; his body touched mine, and I could feel his cock against my stomach, but he kept his weight off me. When he kissed me harder, my legs came up, asking for more access. But he pinned me onto the bed. He squeezed my hips and pushed a finger inside, "Want to do you from behind," he whispered and helped me turn on my stomach. He moved to grab supplies, and I tried to be patient. Then he rewarded me with another kiss, and I felt the coldness of his lubed fingers in my hole. I shuddered for a second, and he kissed my earlobe and my nape while he kept massaging me.

"Is it okay if I fuck you now?" he asked. It wasn't enough lube, but I nodded. He was never going to hurt me. I trusted him.

He grabbed the condom from the table and applied more lube on his shaft. "God, I am desperate for you," he whispered at the back of my ear while he folded my leg up, positioning himself, he pushed his cock inside me.

I opened up to give him more access, and he pushed inside, hitting my prostate making me equally desperate for him.

"Okay?" he asked, gently stroking my hair, and that gesture made my heart swell like he was my lover.

"Yeah," I said. He started moving in and out, and every move gave me an orgasm that never happened to me before. And I kept chasing the feeling with his every move. He finally came, this time before me then he grabbed my cock to help me come with him.

After we were spent, he got off me and lied beside me. We both tried to catch our breath. I turned and lied next to him. Staring at the ceiling, hearing his uneven breath next to me, the moment felt so serene that I closed my eyes to live in it a little longer.

.....

I WOKE UP TO THE SOUND of my phone ring. I looked around and felt a little disoriented for a second. Then I looked at the entrance to the terrace and realized with a panic where I was, and the bright sunlight told me it wasn't night anymore. I quickly sat up on the bed. My phone was again ringing.

"Someone's been calling you non-stop." Mitchel was dressed in his tailor-made grey suit pants and a light-coloured collared shirt. His shirt's buttons were undone when he handed me my phone.

"I..." I started to say, but he interrupted, "Answer it." So, I quickly hit the green icon.

"Where the fuck are you? I have been going crazy. Should I call the cops?" Robbie's panicked voice came through the speaker.

"No, Robbie, I am okay, I am coming home." I said.

"Are you now? I can track your phone. Should I come and get you?" Robbie asked.

"No, Robbie, I am okay. I'll see you soon." I said and watched Mitchel buttoning his shirt and choosing cufflinks.

"Tell me you love me," Robbie said, and I was pretty sure Mitchel heard it because he went utterly still. It was our arrangement; only if I told Robbie that I loved him, he'd know I was in trouble and go to the cops.

"I am okay, Robbie. I'll see you soon," I whispered to him and disconnected the phone.

"I am so sorry, I fell asleep." I quickly started to grab my clothes off the floor. I promptly wore my briefs and started to put on my pants. "I never do that. I don't know what happened. I closed my eyes for a second." I put on my shirt and watched him put on his suit jacket as he turned to face me.

I kept blabbing while he stared at me for a few heart-wrenching seconds, and then he asked," Boyfriend?"

I shut up. I didn't understand the question at first.

"The man on the phone who wouldn't stop calling. Is he your boyfriend?"

"No. No. Robbie is not my boyfriend," I replied.

He scrutinized me like he was detecting me for a lie, and his phone rang, breaking the moment between us.

"Yeah, I am coming. I know Dad's mood," He said to the person on the phone and then turned to me again, "Okay, I have a meeting, gotta go." He held my face and quickly kissed my lips, and before I could savour what had just happened, he walked out the door without a second glance.

I stared after him, "Did he kiss me goodbye?" I said to the cold, empty room.

I turned to get my clothes and noticed he had left his cufflinks drawer open. Those were probably thousands of dollars worth; didn't know who else had access to this room, so I closed the drawer, and it locked automatically. I put on the rest of my clothes, grabbed the envelope from the counter he had left for me, placed the room's key in its place and left.

....

Chapter Seven

Mitchel

I pressed the lobby button on the elevator, and as the elevator's door closed, revealing my reflection on the closed door, a sudden realization hit me, "I kissed him." I said to the empty elevator.

....

"I've been doing this for a while now, Dad. I read through all the papers and matched all the clauses before filing it." I said.

"Then why did it get rejected the first time," he questioned, and I just stared at him, controlling my anger.

"Come on, Dad, there can be many technical reasons. Mitch got it sorted right." Nick defended me.

"And how do you know it's all sorted? What do you know about the business? You decided to walk out." Dad turned on Nick.

"And Mitch decided to stay; that's why you are taking it out on him. Right, Dad?" Nick argued.

"Nick," I warned, there was no arguing with Dad.

"Mitchel is smart. He knows the worth of this business. Unlike your music, it's not a hobby and cannot be taken lightly," Dad's old tricks, constantly comparing us to make the other feel bad.

"Unbelievable, you know how much music I sell daily?" Nick was again falling for Dad's tricks.

"That's because Mitchel decided to fund your hobby; without his support, you'd be singing on the street," Dad poked Nick.

"Dad, just stop it. Both of you." I raised my voice, but it did the trick.

"That's just..." Nick stood up.

"Nick," I warned.

"No, brother, you chose to take this shit, not me," Nick argued.

"Look at the way he talks to me. It's all because of you. You pamper him, you spoiled him," Dad said to me.

"Would you just stop it, Dad? Nick, sit down. And Dad, Nick is getting married. He wanted to tell you, and this is how you act." I said.

"Nick is getting married? You are getting married? Why didn't you tell me?" Dad asked Nick.

"I came to tell you if you were going to let me speak," he sat down again.

"Who are you getting married to?" Dad asked.

"Casey, she sings with me. You've met her at the hotel's anniversary," Nick reminded.

"Oh. That bony girl." Dad commented, and I met Nick's eyes to silently tell him to let it go, "When are you getting married?" He asked.

"Mid-June," Nick replied.

"So next week?"

"No, in two weeks, I think," Nick replied.

"You think? You don't have a date? And what about you, Mitchel? When are you getting married?" Dad turned to me, and my thoughts went to Jean, and I shook my head.

"I am not getting married, Dad," I told him.

"Didn't you have a girlfriend?" He pressed.

"Dad, you are getting old," I remarked.

"I am not getting old. Well, your mother would be happy to see at least one of her sons is getting married." Dad commented and then was lost in his thoughts again. After Mom was gone, he was losing his mind. I wanted him to check with a psychiatrist, but he only got angrier at my suggestion.

....

Dad left with the driver. Nick and I stayed to discuss his wedding date. The wedding date depended on the venue. We had a bunch of hotels, but Casey wanted to get married in a chapel.

"You know how girls are," Nick said. "You are seeing anyone?"

"Umm," I thought of Jean, then I said, "No."

"That wasn't a no, Mitch. Come on, who is she?" he prompted.

"Does it have to be a she?" I said without thinking.

"No way you are seeing a boy," It didn't take Nick long to jump to that conclusion.

"It's a man, but no, I am not seeing him," I corrected.

"Well, you are doing something with him." He said and laughed. I was sure doing a lot with him, but I wasn't dating him.

"It's nothing serious. It's just fun," I said.

"Well, you are talking about him. I wouldn't say it's nothing."

I shrugged. "It's just because he is the first man I've been with. Nothing more to it," I don't know who I was convincing, but I wasn't doing a great job.

"So, you are planning on trying with another man?" He asked.

"I don't know, maybe yeah." I thought about it; maybe that was the solution. Gupta was right. I needed a break from Jean. I can't believe I kissed him this morning like he was my lover.

"Wow, didn't take you for a Casanova," Nick was still teasing.

"I am not a Cassanova. I am not breaking anyone's heart," I said. I may have been with many girls, but the rules were always clear.

"You tell that to that man you are seeing or not seeing," he mocked.

"It's complicated," I said.

He laughed, "Relationships are always complicated."

"That's why I don't do relationships," I told him.

"You don't do relationships, and it's still complicated, then you have a bigger problem, big brother." He said, leaving me with my thoughts. He went to greet Casey at the entrance.

....

Jean

"Here are this month's payments," I told Mikko, handing him most of the money I had earned.

"This is just interest," he said, showing his gold teeth.

"I know. I'll try to pay more." I said.

"Where do you get it, though? Money? Some secret business you want to share with your friends." He smiled. He was not my friend. He was a collector for the loan sharks, and my dad had made the mistake of borrowing money from them. I didn't know about it until he died.

"It's a job I am doing, nothing much," I said.

"Okay, as long as you keep the money coming, we don't care," He said.

I nodded and walked out of his shop.

......

"Paid them all your hard-earned money?" Robbie commented when I got back to the cafe.

"Do I have a choice?" I said, taking the broom from him to clean the floor.

"Yes, you do. You didn't take that loan. Your dad did. He did it for himself. It's got nothing to do with you. Because you are his son, his debt doesn't automatically fall on you. Not to mention illegal debt," Robbie was getting angry on my behalf.

"My father borrowed money to survive. I can't blame him for wanting to make it big." I said.

"Do you think you can ever pay it off? That debt is illegal. There is no paper trail. You have no way of knowing how much you have paid and how much your dad borrowed." he said.

"I know, Robbie, the debt is illegal; that's why I can't do anything," I said and took the broom to clean the bathroom so Robbie could not follow since he had to stay at the counter.

....

I didn't get any Saturday booking. The week was slow, but I was counting on Mitchel. I wanted to see him. I kept thinking about that kiss. He kissed me like I meant something to him. I didn't know much about him, the client's confidentiality and all. If he didn't volunteer the information, I couldn't ask. I checked my phone a few times, and then I called Joe during my break at the cafe. Maybe the system wasn't working, and I didn't get the booking.

"Hey Joe, it's Jean. I'm just checking if you have anything for me this Saturday?"

"Some weeks are slow, you know that." He said.

"What about my Saturday night client?" I couldn't help but ask.

"Oh, sorry, kid, he made a booking but with another lad." My heart sank a thousand miles. "I'll move your profile up and see if I find something. Although you know there is a lot of demand for BDSM, not that I am suggesting it's just more money," he added.

"No, it's okay, just keep my profile up," I told Joe and disconnected.

"He booked someone else," I repeated to myself so I could believe it. I tried to push back my tears. It wasn't a surprise shouldn't have been a surprise. He was just a client who was eventually going to be tired of me. He did get tired of me.

I tried to make myself busy clearing tables and ignoring how my heart had shattered into a million pieces. I did this to myself. I believed I could be anything more to a rich man like him than a whore.

....

Chapter Eight

Mitchel

I picked another man from the catalogue. I was getting too worked up over Jean. Thinking of different ways to please him. It wasn't supposed to be about his pleasure. It was about mine. I really crossed the line when I let him sleep in my bed, and then I kissed him. It wasn't a relationship. I wasn't supposed to pamper him or kiss him like he was my lover. All of this was because I had never been with a man before, so since it was all about fucking a man, there were plenty to fuck. I booked a blond named Charlie. He was 25 years old and slender but didn't have Jean's golden skin. This is what I needed: someone new.

....

Unlike Jean, he didn't knock and used the key card to enter.

He was dressed in all black, "Wow," he looked around the room. "This is huge," he said. Then he walked to me, "Wow, Sir, you are hot; do you want me to call you Sir or Master?" he asked.

"Sir is fine," I said.

"Okay, Sir, where would you like me?" He tried to come closer.

"On your knees," I ordered.

I waited as he got on his knees and started to undo my pants. I waited for that feeling to hit, that arousal that I always felt with Jean. Even that first day when he only suggested that he could give me the service, I felt that arousal. And every time since then, when he knocked on that door, and I told him to come in, I felt it. Now, this man was in front of me on his knees, trying to get the feeling from my cock, but I wasn't feeling it. He took me in his mouth, but other than a sensation of touch, it wasn't doing much. I held his head to direct him, thinking that would help, but his hair felt all wrong; they were not soft like Jean's. They were not bad, but it wasn't the same. My thoughts took me back to Jean and how his mouth felt on my cock and how he looked at me through those long lashes, and my cock stirred.

"That's it." the blond man on his knees said, bringing me back to the present moment. He took me in and out of his mouth, sucking me, but it wasn't doing much.

"Maybe," I said. "Just get up,"

"I was just starting. I'll do better," he said.

"No, let's just—let me fuck you," I said. That should do it. There is no way I wouldn't get aroused fucking someone.

"Sure, how do you want me? I already prepped myself, so you don't have to wait." He started to take off his clothes.

"Okay, but before we start, know that you can stop me at any time. If I hurt you..."

"Oh, you won't hurt me, Sir. I can take pretty much anything. I can easily take two dudes at a time." He took off his shoes and started to take off his pants. And I thought of Jean and how worried he looked when he thought someone else was joining us. "Do you want to hear how I took two cocks? I can give you blow-by-blow. It will surely turn you on."

"No, thank you." I took a sip from my glass of whisky. "Maybe less talking would help," I added.

"I am sorry, Boss." He flushed, and it again reminded me of Jean and how his flushed cheeks looked. "How do you want me?" He asked when he was completely naked.

"On that couch, on your four," I ordered.

"Yes, Boss. I mean, Sir," He said and took the position on the couch. I grabbed the lube and condom and joined him near the couch. His skin was all white, and his hair were unmistakably blond.

I pushed my finger through his crack. He sure was prepared. I hadn't asked him to take a shower. I didn't care; I wanted this to be over. Since when did fucking a prostitute become a chore? I questioned myself. I jacked my cock, in an effort to make it hard.

"Do you want me to suck you again?" He asked.

"No," I said more harshly than I meant to.

"Yes, Boss." He said, remaining in the position.

The only thing that could make me hard at this time was Jean, and I thought of Jean. His soft lips, running my tongue between his lips, feeling his soft, smooth skin in my hands, massaging his warm, tight hole with my fingers. It was enough to make me hard enough to come. I positioned myself and started fucking the blond, but my arousal only came when I thought of Jean. I thought of fucking Jean, I pretended it was him, which he clearly wasn't, but it helped me come.

I handed him his tip and told him to leave while I took the shower.

.....

Jean

Mikko came to the cafe with his men during my shift. "So, this where you work? Cool place," He jumped onto the bar stool.

"Yeah, it's not a month yet. I'll get it next month." I said.

"We are not here for money, we are friends, we just came to see how you make money? Maybe give us half in advance since we are already here." He said.

"I don't have it. I gave you all, and I need to pay the rent," I said.

"So, how will you get it next month?"

"I'll do something. I will get it next month." I promised.

"You'll do something. Okay, then do it. Get it next month," He grabbed all the cookies from the jar and left with his men.

"That's him?" Robbie asked, startling me.

"Yeah, sorry about the cookies. I'll make more." I said.

"Who cares about cookies, Jean? You need to go to the cops."

"What are cops gonna do?" I cleaned the cookie jar.

"They'll put him behind bars," Robbie said.

"No, they'd only get me killed." I took the jar back to the kitchen.

....

"Jean, I told you I'll book if something comes up," Joe said.

"Yeah, I know. I was thinking, what is this role-play? Maybe I can do that." I said.

"The most role-play orders we get is daddy kinks; those older gentlemen have certain preferences; you just don't fit the profile most like their men slimmer and shorter. And then there are BDSM fantasies. It's a bit much for you," he informed.

"Maybe I can do BDSM, something simple," I said.

"No, I don't think you know what that is. I am not putting you in," Joe refused.

"Joe, I did some research. I think I can do it," I insisted.

"It's not just that you can. You have to take pleasure in it. Do you even know what it is?" he questioned.

"Yeah, I know. I want to do it." I said.

"You want to do it?" He asked again.

"I do," I confirmed.

"Okay, I actually have BDSM customers on the waitlist. It's that much in demand. It'll be good pay. But I am doing you a favour here. I don't wanna hear any complaints from customers."

"You won't. I promise. Thank you."

"Okay. Just so we are clear, you asked for it. I didn't make a suggestion." Joe said.

"No, you didn't, Joe." I agreed.

"Okay, I am going to play you a recording with all the information. At the end of the recording, it asks for your consent. If you feel you can't do it, just say no," he informed.

"Okay," I said, and he played the recording. It told me about the safe words Red, Green, Yellow, and company policy. At the end of the recording, I said yes.

I got the notification for booking with the location on my phone right away.

......

I reached the client's apartment and knocked. A giant-sized man opened the door.

"Hello, Sir, I am Jean from Holly High Price."

"Oh bitch, you are beautifuler than your pix." He laughed and grabbed my arm, pulling me inside the apartment. "I am Tito, but you call me master." He pinched my nipple through my shirt, and I winced with pain. "I set it here." He took me to another room, and it looked like something from a horror movie. There were chains and buckles around the bench and bamboos and not-so-comforting dildos and toys. "I got you all for two hours." He said, and I felt his erection behind my hips.

"No," I said, stepping away from him. "I don't wanna do this," I tried to step around him, but he grabbed my wrist and pulled me back, and I felt immense fear at his strength.

"What? Bitch. I paid for you." He growled.

"I know, Sir. But I can't..." I started to explain, but

he slapped me, and I couldn't move.

"What's with the attitude, whore?" He said, grabbing my face. My eyes stung, and my skin felt on fire; he had slapped me with what felt like a hand made of steel.

"You are crying?" He held my face in his big hand and examined it. "For real?" he said. "Oh fuck," he released my wrist and face and stepped back. "I thought you was playing." I couldn't stop my tears. "Oh fuck," he repeated and checked my face again. "Why they send me someone who don't do it?"

"I am sorry." I tried to speak through my tears.

"I ask for someone who like it." He said. "I am calling HHP." He said, grabbing his phone.

"No, please, if you'll complain, they'll fire me," I pleaded.

"What? What is this? You know how much savings I spend on this? I need my money back, they don't do thing to you. It's a mixup. I tell them." He dialled the number, and I heard HHP's automated recording for instructions.

"No, I consented to it. They won't take it lightly." I pleaded.

"Man," he disconnected the call.

"Why you do that?" He asked.

"I needed money. You can fuck me, you can go rough if you want to, I won't complain." I said.

"No, man, just cause I have a kink am not gonna force you. BDSM is for those who enjoys pain." He shook his head.

"I'll tell Joe, my manager, he can get you back my portion of the payment," I said.

"No, you need money, you keep it. I make more, am a plumber, there is always something clogging," he smiled.

I smiled at his generosity.

"You are beautiful you know. Where do I get a guy like you?"

"I am sure HHP has a big list."

"No, I looked," he shook his head. He smiled, then he looked at my mouth. "Can you suck me?" He asked.

"Yes, Master," I smiled and got on my knees in front of him.

......

Tito hadn't complained, but I told Joe BDSM wasn't for me. It sure was good money; it helped me pay my bills, but my rent was coming due, and there was Mikko's payment. Joe said the business would pick up during tourist season, but I didn't get a booking. I picked a shift on Saturday with Robbie for a catering job.

....

Chapter Nine

Mitchel

"It's my bachelor's party, and you are sitting here all alone," Nick complained. He was drunk in tequila shots.

"It's supposed to be your bachelor's party. You are supposed to have fun, not me." I reminded him.

"You know you are the worst host ever," Nick complained.

"I am not your host. Your best man is." I pointed at Gerry, Nick's best friend.

"That's because you opted out. I could have two best men. Speaking of men..." he lowered his voice, although I didn't think anyone could hear us in this music. "What happened to your man?"

"There is no my man," I said, taking a sip from my wine.

"But there is something. You are not just all dopey eyes sitting alone at a party by yourself because of nothing."

"I am not dopey eyes." I laughed at that.

"Come on, tell me what it is?" he whispered as if he was asking me to reveal a company secret.

"Okay, so I had sex with another man."

"Other than your man," he interrupted.

"He's not my man, but yeah him."

"And?"

"And it felt wrong. I couldn't get him out of my head," I said.

"You couldn't get your man out of your head?" He repeated.

"Yeah," I said, giving up on correcting him.

"So, what does it tell you?" he questioned.

I shrugged. "I don't know, Nick. It's probably nothing," I said.

"It's not nothing. I know what to do. You should call him. Ask him on a date." He advised.

"I can't,"

"Why not?"

"It's complicated."

"Then uncomplicate it, man. You are Mitchel Carling; what's so difficult about this man," He said.

"He is not interested in me. I am just money to him."

"My brother, you own a billion-dollar business, you are money to everyone, and so am I, but you know what I have learnt? We don't fall for gold diggers, not really; it's somewhere in our genes that warns us against it, so I am betting my thirty years of experience on it that if you really like this man, then he is not a gold digger. Think real hard, do you really believe it's only your money he is after. I am sure he likes your money; it's part of who you are, but is that all?" He swayed a little, and I grabbed him. "I am okay," he said.

"Are you?" I asked.

"Yeah, it's you who is not okay, Mitch. With love, you gotta take that leap of faith before you miss out on that opportunity of a lifetime because if you don't, he's not gonna wait; he'll find someone else."

"It's not love, Nick." I wanted to convince him, but I wasn't sure myself.

"Yeah, you keep telling yourself that, and your man will be gone. You already cheated on him with another man. So, if I were you, I'd hurry and pray that he never finds out," he tried to take another sip from his glass, but I grabbed it and put it away.

"It's not cheating. I wasn't dating him," I said.

"Sadly, that's not how they see it, see that he doesn't find out," Nick said and moved back to his party.

"Gerry, I said no hookers. Casey will not forgive this." Nick complained, but Gerry dragged him away.

I stepped out of the club to escape the loud music and called HHP. After a long recording, a man named Andrew answered my call. I asked him if I could book Jean for tonight. But he said it was short notice, and Jean was already booked with another client. I disconnected, but I felt a sudden rage at the thought that I was just a client to him. If it wasn't my money, then it was someone else's what can you expect from a whore. He was just a drug I got addicted to. I won't use him. His addiction will eventually wear off.

......

Jean

The catering was for a wedding's after party reception for some pop singer. The kitchen staff prepared all the meals and snacks, and my job was to serve them to guests.

It wasn't a difficult job; everyone was happy to take a snack, and I was told that the budget wasn't a problem for these guys. Looking at the free liquor serving, I'd say so. I was walking around the tables, replacing empty plates, when someone chimed the glass to make an announcement. It was the groom. "Now, I want Mitchel, my big brother, to say something about me since I know Dad has nothing good to say about me, so let's hear you, Mitchel."

Mitchel's name was a painful reminder of rejection. It hurt more than I wanted to admit to myself. I couldn't see who the groom talking to, but it didn't matter. I collected more empty plates and stayed out of guests' way.

"Let's see if there is anything good about you, Nick." His voice came on the mic, and I froze. I knew that voice anywhere. It had taken over my dreams. I turned to see him. He looked perfect in that tuxedo, just like the dream he was. Mr. Presidential Suite, Mitchel, the one who used me, aroused me, made me feel special and then threw me aside and forgot about me like a used toy. The problem was I couldn't blame him because that's what I was to him, just a toy to play with. The toy he paid for. It was my own fault to let him get through my walls, to think that I could be anything more to him than a whore.

"But jokes apart, I am blessed to have a brother like you, Nick..." he was saying. I didn't bother to hear the rest of the speech and collected plates. I had a job to complete.

....

Mitchel

AFTER THE SPEECH AND dinner, everyone started moving to the dance area. And I noticed a server, maybe because he looked like Jean. I was losing my mind over Jean. Now I was seeing him where he wasn't. It was a Saturday, he must be with another client. That thought left a bitter taste in my mouth. I sat at the bar and ordered scotch whisky, my eyes still searching for that server. He had a similar height and body. That's why he reminded me of Jean. I looked around at each server as I sipped my whisky, and my hand froze in midair when my eyes found him. It wasn't someone who looked like Jean. It was Jean. He was carrying a tray, serving Champaign glasses to the guests while giving them his beautiful smile. I got lost watching him and then I realized he wasn't with a client. The realization gave my heart an involuntary thud. I kept my glass at the bar counter and walked straight to him.

"Jean," I said to his back and watched him go still. "Jean," I repeated when he didn't turn.

He gradually turned to face me, but he kept his eyes on the tray in his hand, "Hello, Sir, may I offer you a drink." He said, and my eyes zeroed on the purple wound on his cheek, that he had done a poor job of concealing with makeup.

"Fuck, what happened?" In a trance, I touched his warm cheek, knocking Champagne glasses on the way, partially because I stepped forward and partially because he stepped back.

There was a loud noise of glasses crashing to the ground, and I was pretty sure that everyone was now staring at us, but I couldn't care less. Jean, though cared a lot, he was flustered, frantically looking at guests.

"I am sorry, Sir." He apologized to me when it wasn't his fault. He swiftly got down on his feet and started collecting broken pieces.

"What are you doing? You'll cut yourself." I grabbed his arm and pulled him to his feet, "clean up, here." I ordered the other waiter. I held Jean's wrist and walked him out of the party to the garden, where the wedding ceremony was held in the morning. I knew no one would be there now.

"What are you doing?" Jean tried to pull away from me, but I didn't let go of his hand and pulled him closer.

"What happened to you? Who did this?" I held his face and asked him.

"Nothing, Sir. It was an accident," he pulled away from me to leave, and I grabbed his arm and forced him to stay.

"That doesn't look like any accident; someone has hit you. Who did it? Was it your boyfriend? Robbie? Is it because you slept the night with me?"

"No." He tried to pull away, and I held him in place again.

"Jean, I need an answer," I asked.

"Why? What's it to you?" He questioned, meeting my eyes.

I opened my mouth to answer, but I had no answer. The truth was I was enraged at the thought of someone hurting Jean, and I had this helpless desire to protect him. Instead of saying any of that, I ordered him, "I asked you a question. Just answer me."

"You are not my client anymore. I don't need to answer any of your questions." He tried to move, and I held him in place again.

"I may not be your client, but I am still your boss." I held his shirt pocket where my company logo was engraved, the same logo that was on all my hotels. He lowered his eyes to look at the logo. "Jean, I am not trying to control you." I let go of his arm.

"No, you just boss me around because you can. So, what can I do for you, Sir?" He lowered his eyes and turned an accusatory gaze at me.

"Call me Mitchel," I said, and his eyes went wide with surprise. "I am not your client right now. You are not under any contract or obligation. I just want to know who did this." I touched his cheeks because I couldn't help myself; I wanted to touch him. I missed him, and to my relief, he didn't pull back this time. I wanted to know who did this to Jean so I could hurt him.

Jean closed his eyes. I could see his struggle; he didn't want me to see how hurt he was, and I felt so much rage against the person who had hurt Jean that I never felt against another person in my life.

" A client did it." He finally spoke. "Now, let me go. I have a job to finish." He tried to move past me, but I held him in place.

"Client? How could he hit you? Did you report to the police? What the fuck is HHP doing for your safety? Give me his name," I said.

"I told you, it's nothing. He didn't do anything wrong. I agreed to this.I signed up for BDSM." He said.

"You agreed to this? You told me you don't even like handcuffs, and now you are joining a BDSM club. Why the fuck would you do that?" I objected.

"Why do you think I do anything? I needed money, and it was good pay, and that's all that mattered," He snapped.

"If you needed money, you should have come to me," I said without thinking.

"I should have come to you?" he laughed. "Why do you do that?"

"Do what?" I asked.

"Is this one of your kinks? Do you enjoy playing with me? Well, I do know you enjoy playing with me. So, what is it? Does it turn you on, showing me care, concern, making me feel special, treating me like a lover and then throwing me out like a whore and replacing me with your latest toy?" He was angry. His face was flushed.

"I never threw you out or replaced you." I defended.

"No, you don't throw me out when you are done playing with me; you just tell me to take my money and get the fuck out of there." I winced at his words.

"And by the way, how was the guy you fucked last Saturday, or did you go back to fucking girls again?" He scorned making me feel like an asshole.

"I know you were my client, and I was just a whore to you. But it would have been kinder if you had treated me like one instead of showing me this fake concern, sharing a meal with me, and in bed caring for me like a lover. You were getting to fuck me no matter what. You paid for it. You didn't have to play your fucking games, Sir." he walked by me, and his body brushed against mine, but this time I didn't dare stop him.

....

"Mitch," Nick came and stood before me, searching my face.

"You were right," I said to Nick, "I cheated on him, and he didn't take it lightly."

"So, this is him?" He asked the obvious. "He is a server." It wasn't a question but a comment.

"He is a prostitute," I said, challenging him.

"Are you serious?" Nick asked. "How did you meet him?"

"I hired him," I said.

"For what?" he asked like an idiot.

"What do you think?" I challenged.

He laughed.

"It's funny that I hired a prostitute?" I asked.

"No. I knew you had to be getting it somewhere since you didn't do relationships. I just didn't see my brother falling head over heels for anyone, let alone a man and a prostitute. I mean, wow you don't care what he does, and I can see that you are ready to fight me if I'd even open my mouth against it."

I shook my head and turned to see which way Jean went. "Mitch, I never thought I'd see the day. You shocked the hell out of me." Nick continued, "Man, I write love songs and have never witnessed a love like yours in real life."

"What about your love for your bride?" I asked.

"I do love my Casey, but I don't love her enough to fight for her if she turned out to be a prostitute. You know what I mean." He said, and I glared at him. "I am just being honest, don't let her hear this." He added quickly.

"Shut up, Nick. You were right, it was an opportunity of a lifetime, and I just couldn't get my head out of my ass, and I fucked it up. "I blurted.

"Then fix it, you are Mitchel Carling. How long can he resist your charm? Just a tip: start by apologizing." he gave me a quick hug and left me with my thoughts.

....

I booked Jean again from HHP website. I needed to speak to him and I didn't have any of his information. But HHP cancelled my booking and offered me alternatives. I called HHP and they said Jean was no longer HHP.

Then I called a P.I agency, that was already on my company's payroll to investigate other business that we sign contracts with. Jason Stewart from the P.I agency accepted my case to find information about Jean.

I tried to keep myself busy with work, but I couldn't stop thinking about Jean. He quit HHP, he didn't need money anymore? Or was he just avoiding me. If he needed money, why would he do that. I offered him money, he had a perfect opportunity to come to me, so why wouldn't he?

My phone rang and Jason Stewart, my P.I's name flashed on the screen, I answered it quickly.

"Found anything?" I asked, before Jason could speak.

"I sure did. Jean Marano, 26 years old, lives near Silver Height, works at a Star Bound caffe, most nights and weekends works with HHP. Doesn't have any immediate family. No trouble with the government, pays his bills on time. He is also making regular payments to shylock."

"Shylock?" I asked.

"The loan sharks, moneylenders." he defined, "the lowest kind," he added.

"What for?" I asked.

"That information is difficult to find, Shylocks don't exactly register their businesses with the government, so their transaction are in cash and hard to track."

"Okay," I said.

"Anything else you would like to know?"

"Why, what else you have?" I asked.

"I didn't see any girlfriend but he lives with a guy named Robbie. Roomates, work together." I had heard of Robbie, Jean claimed he wasn't a boyfriend. So I was going to go with that.

"Do you have his address?"

"I do. I'll text you."

"Okay, and Jason, try to find out about these Shylocks and how much does he owe them?"

"Sure thing, Boss. I'll try to find out more about the Shylocks and your boy." He disconnected. I thought about Jean, why was he involved with loan sharks? That's why he went for BDSM, when he didn't like it. It's because I booked someone else. I am an idiot. I thought.

....

Chapter Ten

Jean

I handed money to Mikko. He counted it. "There is two hundred less," he said.

"I know, I'll pay that next week," I said.

"What happened to your job?" He asked. I quit HHP on a whim when I saw that he had booked me again. I didn't want to see him. My heart couldn't take it anymore. I didn't want him to toy with me again. So, I quit without thinking. "Remember what happened the last time you didn't pay." Mikko threatened. I remembered, of course. How could I forget? I was kidnapped from my home, handcuffed and locked in a dungeon until I pleaded and agreed to pay them every month. That fear of being handcuffed and locked in a dark place still haunted my dreams. Being with Mitchel had given me some relief, but the nightmares returned when he replaced me.

"I will pay. Just give me a week," I promised.

"Okay, double interest," he said, smiling with his gold teeth at me.

I nodded and left.

When I got back to the cafe, I called Joe again and pleaded with him to give me the job back. He said I wasn't considered reliable anymore, so I'd have to start at the party scene, which meant more hours and less pay. But I agreed. At least I didn't have to fuck anyone. I used to enjoy my job with HHP. I liked sex, but Mitchel just ruined me. Now, all I wanted was him.

......

Mitchel

I reached the place and met Jason Stewart. "You don't have to do this," Jason said. "I can get my guys to handle it."

"No, I need to do this," I said.

I met a man named Mikko at an old radio shop. It was clearly a money laundry shop. No one bought radios anymore. How cops didn't see it was beyond me.

"Woo man, I got legit business here. No need for you detectives to pay me a personal visit." Mikko complained.

"We are not cops. We are here to talk business." Jason said firmly.

"Business? You think I am dumb? I don't recognize you cops from a mile. With a suit like that, what business you guys got with me?" he said.

"Your cops don't wear a suit like mine; they cannot afford this suit in their salary or my car." I pointed at my five hundred thousand dollar car, and his eyes widened.

"You make a point, Boss. What can I do for you? Need someone killed? Kidnap a girl?" he asked, raising his eyebrows.

"You know a man named Jean Marrano?" I asked.

"Jean," he thought for a second, then his eyes opened with recognition, "that coffee shop bitch, now I know where he gets his money from?" he eyed me, "What? He run away or something? I kidnap him once you know I can do it again," he flashed his gold teeth.

"You kidnapped him?" Without thinking, I grabbed his collar.

His men stepped forward, and Jason took out his gun that I didn't know he was carrying. "Just relax, everyone. I got more men outside than you can count on both hands." Jason warned, pointing his gun at Mikko, and I let go of him, "Woo, man," Mikko gestured his men to hold off. "No need for guns. I didn't touch your bitch. I just handcuffed him, put a little fear; that's how business is done. He owes me money."

"How much?" I asked.

He smiled, "Twenty thousand," I nodded to Jason, "with double interest," he added as an afterthought. I stepped forward, he wasn't tall or strong, but he carried weapons.

"I'll pay you twenty thousand with double interest, but after this, if you come after Jean, I'll make sure to call my friends at the police department, and I promise you this: you won't see outside of the prison before your eightieth birthday," I warned.

"I won't come after your bitch, I just need my money. It's business." He said, showing me his teeth again.

I gestured at Jason, and he handed him the money.

....

"You had men outside, more than he could count on both hands?" I asked Jason when we were in the safety of my car.

"He bought it, right. That's what matters." He said proudly, and I laughed.

"You think he'd still go after Jean?" I asked.

"I hate to break it to you; you stepped into a forbidden territory. And you fed blood to a coyote. If it is someone he'd come after, it's not going to be Jean, but since he knows Jean is your weakness, the sooner you get him out of that lower town, the better," he said as a matter of fact.

....

"Your destination is on the right," the GPS tracker said. I looked at the old building in the central downtown. It was in the lower town. Jason had given me his schedule. At least I knew he wasn't at the cafe, but I didn't know if he was with any client.

After walking those unsanitary stairs, I finally reached his apartment. I knocked at the door.

"Did you forget the key?" I heard Jean's voice through the door. My heart swelled with the knowledge that he was there. I didn't answer, though and knocked again.

"Fuck Robbie, I am going to be late," he opened the door and froze when he saw me. He was halfway dressed; his glittering party shirt buttons were open, and his pants were undone. He looked hot, good enough to eat. I wanted to grab him and kiss his hot mouth.

"I see you are recovering pretty fast from the last I saw you," I remarked.

"Mitchel?" It was the first time he said my name, and I couldn't help but smile.

"You are not going to invite me in?" I asked, and he opened his mouth but was too shocked to speak. "I guess I'll invite myself in," I said, brushing against his hot body as I made my way through the door to his apartment. "Nice place," Not really, but I praised it anyway. At least it looked clean. My compliment, though, had woken him up.

"What the hell are you doing here? How did you find me?" he came to face me.

"I came to see you; that is the answer to your first question, and for the second, I hired a P. I to find you. It was pretty easy," I replied.

"What?" he asked. "Why?" he added.

"I thought I'd ask you out," I said, meeting his eyes.

"You thought you'd ask me out?" he repeated.

"Correction, I want to ask you out. We haven't been on a proper date, so I thought."

"Stop with your fucking games, you are not my client anymore," he cut me off.

"I'm not playing a fucking game with you, Jean. Don't you get it? None of that was a game. I like you. It took me time to realize, but I know now, I want us to be together."

Jean

I JUST STARED AT HIM. I couldn't believe Mitchel was in my apartment. With his expensive suit, his tall height, his perfectly done blond hair and that delightful perfume, he looked out of place in my tiny apartment. He didn't belong here. Mitchel was a dream that my little apartment couldn't handle.

"I want you to leave," I moved to show him the door.

"Jean," he grabbed my wrist, pulling me toward him; he held my face, and I realized how much I craved his touch. "I know I messed up. I was confused, and I didn't do it right. But I want to fix it. I can't stop thinking about you. I want you like I never wanted anything before." He pressed his mouth to mine, and my eyes closed in reaction. I let him kiss me, and I got lost in his taste when he pushed me against the wall and kissed me harder. "You are mine," he whispered. I don't want anyone else to touch you." he whispered against my mouth and kissed down my neck, and I wanted to give in to him. Reality woke me up when the alarm on my phone went off.

"No," I pushed him off. "I can't do this anymore. You can't keep playing with me. I have to go. I have a client." I said, trying to get away.

"No, Jean. You don't have to do this anymore," he said. I looked into his green eyes, which held so much promise. "I know you owed money to loan sharks. I paid it off," he said.

"What?" I pushed him off me, and he let go. "You paid off my loan? How? You don't even know anything about me."

"The man named Mikko that was blackmailing you, I paid him off," He ran his hand through my hair, "now he won't bother you." He said proudly, and I glared at him.

"Who do you think you are?" I raised my voice at him. "You think you can buy anything just because you have money?"

"I didn't say that," he defended, but I cut him off.

"So, now what? You paid off my loan so you can have me all to yourself as your keep?" I burned with anger. He didn't care about me. I was just a thing to him to purchase off the shelf at the right price.

"I didn't say any of that. I asked you on a date, remember?" He retorted.

"Yeah, you said you paid off my loan. Is that how dates work in your high society," I questioned.

"I thought you needed money," He looked puzzled.

"Yes, I need money, and I can make it. I don't need to be your keep," I protested.

"Jean, what the fuck. I didn't say you have to be my keep." He said it like he had a problem with that word.

The phone rang. It was HHP calling. I was late for the client's party. I grabbed the phone, and he took it from my hand and disconnected it.

"Mitchel," I complained.

"I love it when you say my name," he smiled.

I just stared at him.

"Okay, listen. I may have said it wrong. I know how we met. But I am not trying to buy you. I want you, and this money was coming between us, so I paid off your loan. But from now on, we'll do just how you want it, okay. But you can't just keep doing this job," he said, like I agreed, and he used we as if we were in a relationship.

"Why did you hire prostitutes? Why not go out on a date?" I asked the question I always wanted to ask.

He shrugged, and when I just looked at him, waiting for an answer, he said, "I didn't want a relationship, and dating was just a waste of time. Even a one-night stand with a stranger was just too much work, and after a while, it was just..."

"Boring?" I finished his thoughts, and he just looked at me but didn't deny it. "So, what happens when you get bored of me?"

"You didn't let me finish, Jean. I said I didn't want a relationship until I met you. Hell, I'd put more effort for you in our none-dates than I'd ever put in a real date. I never get bored of you. Since I met you, I just can't think of anyone else. I just don't like anyone else in my bed but you. I never felt this way before, so I know it's real. And don't tell me you don't feel the same about me." He challenged.

I lowered my eyes and bit my lips. I didn't want to admit that it was true for me. I didn't like anyone else touching me anymore. I didn't like sex if it wasn't with Mitchel.

"Does it matter what I feel?" I whispered.

"It matters to me because you matter to me, Jean. I am sorry, I hired someone else. I wanted to get you out of my head," I met his eyes again, and he added, "but then I realized you were not in my head; you were in my heart, and there was no getting you out."

I searched his dark green eyes because I couldn't make myself believe that this was not a dream and Mitchel was saying all those things to me, and then he kissed me again.

"We can't be together. You and me are not the same; it's not possible." I rationalized, but I couldn't push him away.

"Yeah, you are right. We sure are not the same. I can never have your dancing skills. And God, the way you flex those legs," He touched my hips, and it was that easy for him to arouse me.

"Mitchel, I am nothing. And you are ..." I shook my head, my eyes stung with the thought that I couldn't have Mitchel even if he wanted me. "I don't fit in your life, your social circle. I am no match for you," I said.

"Okay, If that's the problem, I have a solution," Mitchel said cheerfully.

"Solution?" I asked.

"Yeah," he took out the ring from his little finger that he always wore and grabbed my hand. Putting it on my ring finger, he said. "Let's get married."

"No," I said, pulling my hand back.

"No?" he searched my eyes, and he looked worried, and I felt a strong desire to take away all his worries.

"No, I mean, like, what?" I asked.

"Is it a yes or no?" he questioned.

"I don't understand," I said.

"Okay, see." he rested his hips on the study table and pulled me between his legs. "I am one hundred percent certain that I'd never get bored of you, and I want you all to myself. Exclusive. You are worried about the money wedge between us and our status not being the same. So, if we get married, then I get to have you all to myself without ever worrying about any disgusting labels that people might throw at us, and you won't have to worry about our status being different because it will become the same since after marriage all my money will be yours too. And if it doesn't work out and you get bored of me because I know I'd never get bored of you, then you get to keep half of the money, so now there is no risk," he said with determination, and I just stared at him.

"Are you out of your mind?" I said in disbelief.

"Since I met you, I think a little." He smiled, pulled me even closer and pressed a kiss on my neck.

"This is not right," I argued.

"Jean, don't you get it. I don't care about the money. I care about you. I want you to feel safe and never worry about a dime in your life." He looked into my eyes to make sure I believed him.

"What about your family? Don't they want you to marry someone of your status?" I asked.

He smiled, grabbed my hand and rubbed that ring he had just put on my finger, "It was my mom's ring. She didn't come from a wealthy family, but my dad fell in love with her. It took my dad some time convincing my mom, but she accepted him. I am not worried about my family or anyone else. I don't care what anyone else thinks. I never did. I love you, and you are all that matters to me." He said, kissing my lips. I was still hung on his words. He said, 'I love you.'

"Mitchel," I breathed out with need.

"Please say yes," he whispered, kissing my ear.

"Yes," I heard myself say.

And he moved back to look into my eyes.

"Yes?" he asked with a grin.

"Yes," I nodded.

"I love you, and I can't have enough of you," He repeated and kissed me, pushing his tongue inside my mouth, making me close my eyes.

"I love you," I breathed the words between his kisses, and he pulled me on his lap, pressing my body against his.

Holding On to Him
Next Book: A sequal to *Revelling in Him*

Synopsis

MM ROMANCE. STEAMY Gay Romance.

They were in love. It should have been enough. Love can conquer any obstacle; that's what most romance novels promise, so it must be true. The love just had to be strong enough. Was Mitchel and Jean's love strong enough to withstand this social class difference between them? It was supposed to be them against the world, but then why it felt like they were battling against each other? Each wanted their place in the house while maintaining their place in the heart of the other.

Mitchel never thought he could ever fall in love with anyone as he had fallen for Jean. Jean was forever. He was sure of it. There was nothing wrong with Jean. He was perfect the way he was. Mitchel didn't care what social class Jean belonged to or what he used to do for a living. But Mitchel didn't think there was any need to advertise that past. To start a new life together, Jean had to give up his old one; Mitchel thought it was obvious from the start.

The relationships are about compromises, and lately, it felt like that's all Jean was doing. Compromising. Adjusting to Mitchel Carling's world. Jean understood why he couldn't talk about his past with people from Mitchel's social circle, but Mitchel didn't have to direct his every word. Did he think Jean was that stupid not to know what to say to whom? Even though he'd never say it, Jean started to feel Mitchel was ashamed of him.

Follow A.B Julian for updates on the next book and release date. https://abjulian.com

About the Author

A.B Julian has an MA in Education and Psychology from the University of Toronto. Currently lives on an island with three cats. Besides teaching elementary students, A.B Julian enjoys reading and writing MM romance.

Read more at https://abjulian.com.